Moving

written and photographed
by
Mia Coulton

Danny's Big Adventure #6

Moving

Published by:
MaryRuth Books, Inc.
18660 Ravenna Road
Chagrin Falls, OH 44023
www.maryruthbooks.com

Text copyright © 2012 Mia Coulton
Illustrations copyright © 2012 Mia Coulton

Editor: Heidi Makela

First Edition
10 9 8 7 6 5 4 3 2 1

ISBN 978-1-933624-90-7

SPC/0412/101392

For Joey

Contents

Time to Move

Danny couldn't sleep.

He got up and sat by his window.

He stared outside.

It was early morning.

The sun was just starting to rise in the east.

He watched a couple of early morning walkers pass his house.

He watched two squirrels chase each other up a tree.

In a few hours, Danny would be watching a moving van pull into the driveway.

In a few hours, Danny would have to say goodbye to everything that gave him comfort.

Danny was moving out of the red house in the middle of the block.

Danny had lived in the red house for all of his life.

He felt sad.

He felt scared.

He felt sick to his stomach.

He felt it was just not fair
that no one asked him about
the move.
He did not want to move,
but he did not have a choice
in the matter.

Before the moving van arrived,
Danny wanted to stop
at Abby's house.
Abby was Danny's best friend.
She lived around the corner
from Danny.

Danny and Abby played together
every day.

Danny wanted Abby never
to forget him. He wanted her
to remember the special times
they had shared.

So Danny made a memory jar.

The Memory Jar

Inside the memory jar were a yellow ribbon, a birthday hat, some burrs and photos.

The yellow ribbon was the ribbon Danny wore around his neck when he was a puppy.

Danny and Abby first met when they both were puppies.
They would run and tumble to the ground. Abby would grab hold of the ribbon and try to pull it off Danny.
He was sure she would remember the yellow ribbon.

One day Danny and Abby
were playing in the park.
They took a shortcut home.
They ran through
tall grass and bushes.
When they got home, they had
burrs all over their fur. It was
hard to get the burrs
out of their fur.

Under his bed, Danny had found
a clump of the burrs stuck
to his bed.

The burrs were from that day in
the park.

Danny had put the burrs in
the memory jar.

He was sure Abby would
remember that day in the park.

Danny had put some photos
in the memory jar, too.
The photos were of Danny
and Abby when they dressed in
"make believe" clothes.
They were dressed up as pirates.
They were dressed up as a doctor
and a nurse.
They were dressed up as a king
and a princess.
He was sure Abby would
remember all those
"make believe" days.

19

Danny carefully put the memory jar in a paper bag with a sturdy handle and walked to Abby's house.

He left the memory jar at her front door.

He didn't want to stay and say
goodbye. He didn't want to see her
one last time. He didn't want Abby
to see him cry. He was told moving
was going to be a new adventure.
He was told he would like
the new house.

Danny started to walk home.

When he rounded the corner,

he saw the moving van

in front of his house.

He stopped.

He turned.

He looked back

towards Abby's house

one last time.

Then he took a deep breath

and continued to walk home.

Old House

BEE
Room 3

DANNY
Room 3

OLD PHOTOS
Attic

BOOKS
Den

POTS and PANS
Kitchen

Danny went into the house.

He saw boxes stacked and ready

to be loaded into the moving van.

Then Danny saw his name on one

of the boxes.

"Funny," he thought, "everything

that's mine fits into one box!"

He noticed under his name was

written "Room 3".

Danny wondered, "What does

"Room 3" mean?"

He walked into the dining room.

It was empty. It all looked so

different, smaller somehow.

He walked into the living room.

He saw his window,

the window he had spent so

many hours sitting

in front of, looking outside.

He knew he would miss

his window, but he was told there

would be four new and bigger

windows to look out of all day.

Danny saw a ramp going out the front door.

He took a look.

The ramp went right into the moving van.

Danny walked up the ramp and into the moving van.

Then he went down the ramp and back into the house.

He thought it was fun to walk up and down the ramp of the moving van.

Honk! Honk!

It was time to get out of the moving van. It was time to get in the car. It was time to leave the old red house and go to the new red house.

New House

The new house was big and red.

Danny was happy it was red.

His old house was red, now his

new house was red.

The yard was big. There was

a fence around the yard.

Danny was happy about that, too.

The fence would keep him close to home. He wouldn't be able to wander away. The fence would keep him safe.

Danny slowly entered
the new house.

The first thing
he saw in the new house
was a door with a sticker
that said "Room 3".

He pushed open the door
and peeked inside the room.

He saw the box with his name.

He knew this was where
he would be sleeping.

He went into another room.

He saw four big windows.

He walked over to the windows
and sat down. Danny looked
out the windows and thought,
"These must be my
new four big windows.

I can see far, far away.

There is so much to see.

I can see a lake.

I can see birds,
and I can see a cat!

Maybe the cat will be my friend?"

Danny ran outside.

He wanted to play with the cat.

The cat was sitting on the fence.

"Cat, cat, play with me!"

Danny barked.

The cat did not want to play.

The cat jumped off the fence

and ran into the yard.

"I bet the cat will come back and

play tomorrow. I bet the cat will

be my new friend,"

Danny said to himself.

Later that night,

Danny settled into his bed

in Room 3.

He snuggled with Bee,

just like he always did

in his old house.

Dad read a book to him,

just like he always did

in his old house.

Dad said goodnight to him,

just like he always did

in his old house.

Danny no longer felt scared.

He wasn't happy but he wasn't
sad either.

He went to bed thinking about
all he had done on moving day
and the new adventures he would
have in the new red house.